THE SOUTH ALSO EXISTS

Hugo Chavez

THE SOUTH ALSO EXISTS

Published in 2005 by
LeftWord Books
2254/2A, Shadi Khampur
New Ranjit Nagar
New Delhi 110008
INDIA
www.leftword.com

Digital print edition, March 2020

LeftWord Books is a division of
Naya Rasta Publishers Pvt. Ltd.

ISBN 978-81-87496-56-4

Contents

Either We Invent
Or We Err

[Speech at the United Nations, New York City, USA:
September 16, 2005.]

Your Excellencies, friends, good afternoon:

The original purpose of this meeting has been completely distorted. The imposed centre of debate has been a so-called reform process that overshadows the most urgent issues, what the peoples of the world claim with urgency: the adoption of measures that deal with the real problems that block and sabotage the efforts made by our countries for real development and life.

Five years after the Millennium Summit, the harsh reality is that the great majority of estimated goals – which were very modest, indeed – will not be met.

We pretended to reduce by half the 842 million hungry people by the year 2015. At the current rate that goal will be achieved by the year 2215. Who in this audience will be there to celebrate it? That is only if the human race is able to survive the destruction that threatens our natural environment.

We had claimed the aspiration of achieving universal primary education by the year 2015. At the current rate that goal will be reached after the year 2100. Let us prepare, then, to celebrate it.

Friends of the world, this takes us to a sad conclusion: The United Nations has exhausted its model, and it is not all about reform. The 21st century claims deep changes that will only be possible if a new organization is founded. This UN does not work. We have to say it. It is the truth. These transformations – the ones Venezuela is referring to – have, according to us, two phases: The immediate phase and the aspiration phase, a utopia. The first is framed by the agreements that were signed in the old system. We do not run away from them. We even bring concrete proposals in that model for the short term. But the dream of an ever-lasting world peace, the dream of a world not ashamed by hunger, disease, illiteracy, extreme necessity, needs – apart from roots – to spread its wings to fly. We need to spread our wings and fly. We are aware of a

frightening neo-liberal globalization, but there is also
the reality of an interconnected world that we have
to face not as a problem but as a challenge. We
could, on the basis of national realities, exchange
knowledge, integrate markets, interconnect, but at
the same time we must understand that there are
problems that do not have a national solution: radio-
active clouds, world oil prices, diseases, warming
of the planet or the hole in the ozone layer. These
are not domestic problems. As we stride toward a
new United Nations model that includes all of us
when they talk about the people, we are bringing
four indispensable and urgent reform proposals to
this Assembly: first, the expansion of the Security
Council in its permanent categories as well as the
non permanent categories, thus allowing new
developed and developing countries as new permanent and non-permanent categories. Second, we need
to assure the necessary improvement of the work
methodology in order to increase transparency, not
to diminish it. Third, we need to immediately
suppress – we have said this repeatedly in Venezuela

for the past six years – the veto in the decisions taken by the Security Council, that elitist trace is incompatible with democracy, incompatible with the principles of equality and democracy.

And fourth, we need to strengthen the role of the Secretary General; his/her political functions regarding preventive diplomacy, that role must be consolidated. The seriousness of all problems calls for deep transformations. Mere reforms are not enough to recover that "we" all the peoples of the world are waiting for. More than just reforms we in Venezuela call for the foundation of a new United Nations, or as the teacher of Simón Bolívar, Simón Rodríguez said: "Either we invent or we err."

At the Porto Alegre World Social Forum last January different personalities asked for the United Nations to move outside the United States if the repeated violations to international rule of law continue. Today we know that there were never any weapons of mass destruction in Iraq. The people of the United

States have always been very rigorous in demanding the truth from their leaders; the people of the world demand the same thing. There were never any weapons of mass destruction; however, Iraq was bombed, occupied and it is still occupied. All this happened over the United Nations. That is why we propose to this Assembly that the United Nations should leave a country that does not respect the resolutions taken by this same Assembly. Some proposals have pointed to Jerusalem as an international city as an alternative. The proposal is generous enough to propose an answer to the current conflict affecting Palestine. Nonetheless, it may have some characteristics that could make it very difficult to become a reality. That is why we are bringing a proposal made by Simón Bolívar, the great Liberator of the South, in 1815. Bolívar proposed then the creation of an international city that would host the idea of unity.

We believe it is time to think about the creation of an international city with its own sovereignty, with its own strength and morality to represent all nations of the world. Such international city has to balance five centuries of unbalance. The headquarters of the United Nations must be in the South.

Ladies and gentlemen, we are facing an unprecedented energy crisis in which an unstoppable increase of energy is perilously reaching record highs, as well as the incapacity of increase oil supply and the perspective of a decline in the proven reserves of fuel worldwide. Oil is starting to become exhausted.

For the year 2020 the daily demand for oil will be 120 million barrels. Such demand, even without counting future increments – would consume in 20 years what humanity has used up to now. This means that more carbon dioxide will inevitably be increased, thus warming our planet even more.

Hurricane Katrina has been a painful example of the cost of ignoring such realities. The warming of the oceans is the fundamental factor behind the demolishing increase in the strength of the hurricanes we have witnessed in the last years. Let this occasion be an outlet to send our deepest condolences to the people of the United States. Their people are brothers and sisters of all of us in the Americas and the rest of the world.

It is unpractical and unethical to sacrifice the human race by appealing in an insane manner to the validity of a socioeconomic model that has a galloping destructive capacity. It would be suicidal to spread it and impose it as an infallible remedy for the evils that are caused precisely by them.

Not too long ago the President of the United States went to an Organization of American States' meeting to propose Latin America and the Caribbean to increase market-oriented policies, open market policies – that is neo-liberalism – when it is precisely the fundamental cause of the great evils and the great tragedies currently suffered by our people: neo-liberal capitalism, the Washington Consensus. All this has generated a high degree of misery, inequality and infinite tragedy for all the peoples on his continent.

What we need now more than ever Mr. President is a new international order. Let us recall the United Nations General Assembly in its sixth extraordinary session period in 1974, 31 years ago, where a new International Economic Order action plan was adopted, as well as the States Economic Rights and Duties Charter by an overwhelming majority, 120 votes for the motion, 6 against and 10 abstentions. This was the period when voting was possible at the United Nations. Now it is impossible to vote. Now they approve documents such as this one that I denounce on behalf of Venezuela as null, void and illegitimate. This document [The Draft Outcome Document to reform the UN, September 13, 2005] was approved violating the current laws of the United Nations. This document is invalid! This document should be discussed; the Venezuelan government will make it public. We cannot accept an open and shameless dictatorship in the United Nations. These matters should be discussed and that is why I petition my colleagues, heads of states and heads of governments, to discuss it.

I just came from a meeting with President Néstor Kirchner and well, I was pulling this document out; this document was handed out five minutes before – and only in English – to our delegation. This document was approved by a dictatorial hammer that I am here denouncing as illegal, null, void and illegitimate.

Hear this, Mr. President: if we accept this, we are indeed lost. Let us turn off the lights, close all doors and windows! That would be unbelievable: us accepting a dictatorship here in this hall.

Now more than ever – we were saying – we need to retake ideas that were left on the road such as the proposal approved at this Assembly in 1974 regarding a New Economic International Order.

Article 2 of that text confirms the right of states to nationalize the property and natural resources that belonged to foreign investors. It also proposed to create cartels of raw material producers. In Resolution 3021, May, 1974, the Assembly expressed its will to work with utmost urgency in the creation of a New Economic International Order based on – listen carefully, please – "the equity, sovereign equality, interdependence, common interest and cooperation among all states regardless of their economic and social systems, correcting the inequalities and repairing the injustices among developed and developing countries, thus assuring present and future generations, peace, justice and a social and economic development that grows at a sustainable rate."

The main goal of the New Economic International Order was to modify the old economic order conceived at Breton Woods.

We the people now claim – this is the case of

Venezuela – a new international economic order. But it is also urgently a new international political order. Let us not permit a few countries to reinterpret the principles of International Law in order to impose new doctrines such as "pre-emptive warfare." Oh do they threaten us with that pre-emptive war! And what about the "Responsibility to Protect" doctrine? We need to ask ourselves: who is going to protect us? How are they going to protect us?

I believe one of the countries that require protection is precisely the United States. That was shown painfully with the tragedy caused by Hurricane Katrina; they do not have a government that protects them from the announced nature disasters, if we are going to talk about protecting each other; these are very dangerous concepts that shape imperialism, interventionism as they try to legalize the violation of national sovereignty. The full respect towards the principles of International Law and the United Nations Charter must be, Mr. President, the keystone for international relations in today's world and the base for the new order we are currently proposing.

It is urgent to fight, in an efficient manner, international terrorism. Nonetheless, we must not use it as an excuse to launch unjustified military aggressions which violate international law. Such has been the doctrine following September 11. Only a true and close cooperation and the end of the double discourse that some countries of the North apply regarding terrorism could end this terrible calamity.

In just seven years of the Bolívarian Revolution, the people of Venezuela can claim important social and economic advances.

One million four hundred and six thousand Venezuelans learned to read and write. We are 25 million total. And the country will – in a few days – be declared illiteracy-free territory. And three million Venezuelans, who had always been excluded because of poverty, are now part of primary, secondary and higher studies.

Seventeen million Venezuelans – almost 70 per cent of the population – receive, for the first time, universal healthcare, including medicines, and in a few years, all Venezuelans will have free access to an excellent healthcare service. More than a million seven hundred tons of food is channeled to over 12 million people at subsidized prices, almost half the population. One million gets them completely free, as they are in a transition period. More than 700,000 new jobs have been created, thus reducing unemployment by 9 per cent. All of this amid internal and external aggressions, including a coup d'état and an oil industry shutdown organized by Washington. Regardless of the conspiracies, the lies spread by powerful media outlets, and the permanent threat of the empire and its allies. They even call for the assassination of a president. The only country where a person is able to call for the assassination of a head of state is the United States. Such was the case of a Reverend called Pat Robertson, very close to the White House: he called for my assassination and he is a free person. That is international terrorism!

We will fight for Venezuela, for Latin American integration and the world. We reaffirm our infinite faith in humankind. We are thirsty for peace and justice in order to survive as a species. Simón Bolívar, founding father of our country and guide of our revolution, swore to never allow his hands to be idle or his soul to rest until he had broken the shackles which bound us to the empire. Now is the time to not allow our hands to be idle or our souls to rest until we save humanity.

[Translated by Néstor Sánchez.]

The Spirit of the South

[Speech at the XII G-15 Summit, Caracas, Venezuela: March 1, 2004.]

Welcome to this land washed by the waters of the Atlantic Ocean and the Caribbean Sea, crossed by the magnificent Orinoco River. A land crowned by the perpetual snow of the Andean mountains . . . !

A land overwhelmed by the never-ending magic of the Amazon forest and its millenary chants . . . !

Welcome to Venezuela, the land where a patriotic people has taken over again the banners of Simón Bolívar, its Liberator, whose name is well known beyond these frontiers!

As Pablo Neruda said in his "Song to Bolívar":

Our Father thou art in Heaven,
In water, in air
In all our silent and broad latitude
Everything bears your name, Father in our dwelling:
Your name raises sweetness in sugarcane
Bolívar tin has a Bolívar gleam
The Bolívar bird flies over the Bolívar volcano

The potato, the saltpeter, the special shadows,
The brooks, the phosphorous stone veins
Everything comes from your extinguished life
Your legacy was rivers, plains, bell towers
Your legacy is our daily bread, oh Father.

Yes, ladies and gentlemen: Bolívar, another "Quixote, but not mad" (as Napoleon Bonaparte had already called Francisco de Miranda, the universal man from Caracas), who on this very same land of South America tried to unite the Rising Republics in a single, strong and free Republic.

In his letter to Jamaica in 1815, Bolívar said talking about the Panama isthmus and his idea of convening there an Amphictyonic Congress:

> I wish one day we would have the opportunity to install there an august congress with the representatives of the Republics, Kingdoms and Empires to debate and discuss the highest interests of Peace and War with the countries of

the other three parts of the world.

Bolívar reveals himself as an anti-imperialist leader, in the same historic perspective that 140 years after that insightful letter at Kingston materialized in the Bandung Conference in April 1955. Inspired by Nehru, Tito and Nasser, a group of important leaders gathered at this conference to face great challenges and expressed their wish of not being involved in the East-West conflict and rather work together toward national development. This was the first key milestone: the first Afro-Asian conference, the immediate precedent of the Non-Aligned Countries that gathered 29 Heads of State and from which the "Conscience of the South" was born.

Two events of great political significance occurred in the 1960s: the creation of the Non-Aligned Movement in Belgrade in 1961 and the Group of the 77 in 1964. Two milestones and a clear historic trend: the need of the self-awareness of the South and of acting together in a world reality characterized by imbalance and unequal exchange.

In the 70s a proposal, arising from the IV Summit of Heads of State of the Non-Aligned Countries in Algiers in 1973, becomes important: the need to create a new international economic order. In 1974 the UN Assembly ratified this proposal, which maintains full effectiveness, but ended up becoming a mere historical reference.

Two events that were very important for the struggles in the South occurred during the 80s: the creation of the Commission of the South in Kuala Lumpur in 1987 under the leadership of Julius Nyerere, the unforgettable fighter of Tanzania and the world.

Two years later, in September 1989, the Group of the 15 was born within the framework of the meeting of the Non-Aligned Countries, with the purpose of strengthening South-South cooperation.

In 1990, the South-Commission submitted its

strategic proposal: "A Challenge for the South". And later on . . . later on came the Flood with the fall of the Berlin Wall and the implosion of the Soviet Union; unipolarity appears and the "happy 90s" arrived, as Joseph Stiglitz said.

All those struggles, ideas and proposals sunk in the neo-liberal Flood and the world began to witness the so-called "end of history" and the triumphant chant of the neo-liberal globalization, which today, besides an objective reality, is a weapon of mani-pulation intended to force us to passiveness faced to an Economic World Order that excludes our South countries and condemns them to the never-ending role of producers of wealth and recipients of leftovers.

Never before had the world seen such tremendous scientific-technical potential, such a capacity to generate wealth and well being. Authentic techno-logical wonders that have made any place in the world to be always close with regard to distances and communications and have not been capable of bringing well-being for everybody, but only for a meager 15 per cent living in the countries of the North.

Globalization has not brought so-called interdependence, but an increase in dependency. Instead of wealth globalization, there is poverty wide spreading. Development has not become general, or been shared. To the contrary, the abyss between North and South is now so huge, that the unsustainability of the current economic order and the blindness of the people who try to justify continuing to enjoy opulence and waste, are evident.

The face of this world economic order of globalization with a neo-liberal sign is not only the internet, virtual reality or the exploration of the space.

This face can also be seen, and with a greater dramatic character in the countries of the South, in the 790 millions of people who are starving, 800 millions of illiterate adults, 654 million human beings who live today in the south and who will not grow older than 40 years of age. This is the harsh and hard face of the work economic order dominated by the neo-liberalism and seen every year in the South, the death of over 11 millions of boys and girls below 5 years of age caused by illnesses that are practically always preventable and curable and who die at the appalling rate of over 30,000 everyday, 21 every minute, 10 each 30 seconds. In the South, the proportion of children suffering of malnutrition reaches up to 50 per cent in quite a few countries, while according to the FAO, a child who lives in the First World will consume throughout his or her life, the equivalent to what 50 children consume in an underdeveloped country.

The great possibilities that a globalization of solidarity and true cooperation could bring to all people in the world through the scientific-technical wonders, has been reduced by the neo-liberal model to this grotesque caricature full of exploitation and social injustice.

Our countries of the South have repeated a thousand times that the sole and true "science" capable of ensuring development and well-being for everybody, without exception, was synthesized in leaving the markets operate without regulation, privatizing everything and creating the conditions for transnational capital investment, and banning the State from intervening the economy.

Almost the magic and wonderful philosopher's stone!

Neo-liberal thought and politics were created in the North to serve their interests, but it should be highlighted that they have never been truly applied there, but they have been spread throughout the South in the past two decades and reached the disastrous category of a single thought.

Through the application of the sole thought, the world economy as a whole grew less than in the three decades between 1945 and 1975, when the Keynesian theories promoting market regulation through State intervention were applied. The gap separating the North and the South continued to grow, not only with regard to economic indicators, but also in the strategic sector of access to knowledge, from which the fundamental possibility of integral development in our times arises.

The countries of the North, with 15 per cent of the world population, account for over 85 per cent of internet users and control 97 per cent of the patents. These countries have an average of over 10 years of schooling, while in the countries of the South schooling hardly reaches 3.7 years and in many countries is even lower.

The tragedy of underdevelopment and poverty in Africa, whose historic roots lay in colonialism and the slavery of millions of its children, is now reinforced by the neo-liberalism from the North. In this region, the rate of infant mortality in children under 1 year of age is 107 per thousand children, while in the developed countries this rate is 6 per thousand children; also, life expectancy is 48 years, thirty years less than in countries of the North.

In Asia, economic growth in some countries has been remarkable, but the region, as a whole, still presents a delay with regard to the North in basic economic and social development aspects.

We are, dear friends, in Latin America, the favorite scenario of the neo-liberal model in the past decades. Here, neo-liberalism reached the status of a dogma and was applied with greatest severity.

Its catastrophic results can be easily seen and are the explanation for the growing and uncontrollable social protest that the poor people and the excluded people of Latin America have been expressing, every day more vigorously, for some years now, claiming their right to life, to education, to health, to culture, to a decent living as human beings.

Dear friends:

I saw with my own eyes, a day like today but exactly 15 years ago, the 27th of February 1989, when an intense day of protest broke out on the streets of Caracas against the neo-liberal package of the International Monetary Fund and ended in a real massacre known as "The Caracazo".

The neo-liberal model promised Latin Americans greater economic growth, but during the neo-liberal years growth has not even reached half the growth achieved in the 1945–1975 period with different politics.

The model recommended the most strict financial liberalization and exchange freedom to achieve a greater influx of foreign capital and greater stability. But in neo-liberal years the financial crises have been more intense and frequent than ever before, the external regional debt, non-existent at the end of the Second World War, amounts today to 750 billion dollars, the per capita highest debt in the world and in several countries is equal to more than half the GDP. Only between 1990 and the year 2002, Latin America made external debt payments amounting to 1 trillion 528 billions of dollars, which duplicates the amount of the current debt and represented an annual average payment of 118 billions. That is, we pay the debt every 6.3 years, but this evil burden continues to be there, unchanging and inextinguishable.

It is a never-ending debt!

Obviously, this debt has exceeded the normal and reasonable payment commitments by any debtor and has turned into an instrument to undercapitalize our countries additionally to the imposition of socially adverse measures that subsequently generate powerful politically destabilizing factors for the governments that insist in their implementation.

We were asked to be ultraliberal in trade and to lift

any barrier, which may obstruct the imports coming from the North, but the oral champions of free trade actually are the champions in the praxis of protectionism. The North spends 1 billion dollars a day in practicing what has been banned from doing, that is, subsidizing inefficient products.

I want to tell you – and this is true and verifiable – that each cow grazing in the European Union receives in its four stomachs 2.20 dollars a day in subsidies, thus having a better situation than 2.5 billion poor people in the South who hardly survive with an income less than 2 dollars a day.

With the FTAA, the government of the United States wants us to reach a zero tariff situation in their benefit and wants us to give away our markets, our oil, our water resources and biodiversity, in addition to our sovereignty, whereas walls of subsidies for agriculture keep access closed to the market of that country. It is a peculiar way of relieving the huge commercial deficit of the United States, to do exactly the contrary to what they present as a sacred principle in economic policy.

Neo-liberalism promised Latin American people that if they accepted the demands of the multinational capital, investments would overflow the region. Indeed, the incoming capital increased. A portion to buy state-owned companies sometimes at bargain prices, another portion was speculative capital to seize the opportunities involved in the financial liberalization environment.

The neo-liberal model promised that after a painful adjustment period necessary to deprive the State of its regulatory power over the economy and liberalize trade and finance, wealth would spread over Latin America and the long-lasting history of poverty and underdevelopment would be left behind. But the painful and temporary adjustment became permanent and appears to become everlasting. The results cannot be concealed.

Taking 1980 as the conventional year of the commencement of the neo-liberal cycle, by that time around 35 per cent of the Latin American population were poor. Two decades thereafter, 44 per cent of Latin American men and women are poor. Poverty is particularly cruel to children. It is a sad reality that in Latin America most of the poor people are children and most children are poor. In the late 90s, the Economic Commission for Latin America reported that 58 per cent of children under 5 were poor, as well as 57 per cent of children with ages ranging from 6 to 12.

Poverty among children and teenagers tends to reinforce and perpetuate inequalities of access to education, as shown by a survey conducted by the Inter-American Development Bank on 15 countries where householders in 10 per cent of the population with the highest income had an average schooling of 11 years, whereas among householders in 30 per cent of the lowest income population such average was 4 years.

Neo-liberalism promised wealth. And poverty has spread, thus making of Latin America the most unequal region over the world in terms of income distribution. In the region, the wealthiest 10 per cent of the population – those who are satisfied with neo-liberalism and feel enthusiastic about the FTAA – receive nearly 50 per cent of the total income, where the poorest 10 per cent – those who never appear in high class society chronicles of the oligarchic mass media – barely receive 1.5 per cent of such total income.

This exploitation model has turned Latin America and the Caribbean into a social bomb ready to explode, should anti-development, unemployment and poverty keep increasing.

Even though the social struggles are growing sharp and even some governments have been overthrown by uprisings, we are told by the North that the neo-liberal reform has not yielded good results because it has not been implemented in full.

So, they now intend to recommend the formula of suicide. But we know, brothers and sisters, that countries do not commit suicide. The people of our countries awake, stand up and fight!

As a conclusion, their Excellencies, because of its injustice and inequality, the economic and social order of neo-liberal globalization appears to be a dead-end street for the South.

Therefore, the passive acceptance of the rules of expulsion imposed by this economic and social order cannot be the behavior to be exercised by the Heads of State and Government who have the highest responsibility before our peoples.

The history of our countries does not admit any doubt – passivity and grieving are useless, instead, the joined and firm action is the sole conduct enabling the South to rise from its sad role of exploited and humiliated rearguard.

Thanks to the heroic struggle against colonialism, the developing countries broke the economic and social order condemning them to the condition of exploited colonies. Colonialism was not defeated by the accumulations of tears of sorrow or by the repentance of colonialists, but for centuries of heroic fights for independence and sovereignty in which the resistance, tenacity and sacrifice of our peoples worked wonders.

Here, in South America, this year we are commemorating 180 years of the heroic deeds of the Battle of Ayacucho, where the people joined and became a liberating army after almost 20 years of revolutionary wars under the leadership of José de San Martin, Bernardo O'Higgins, José Inacio Abreu e Lima, Simón Bolívar and Antonio José de Sucre, expelling the Spanish empire hitherto extended from the warm Caribbean beaches to the cold lands of Patagonia, thus ending 300 years of colonialism.

Today, *vis-à-vis* the obvious failure of neo-liberalism

and the great threat that the International Economic Order represents for our countries, it is necessary to retake the Spirit of the South.

That is where this Summit in Caracas is headed.

I propose to re-launch the G-15 as a South Integration Movement rather than a group. A movement for the promotion of all possible trends, who walks towards the Non-aligned Movement, the Group of 77, China . . . The entirely whole South!

I propose that we retake the proposals of the 1990 South Commission:

Why not focus our attention and our political actions to the proposals for granting several thousand "Grants of the South" per year to students from underdeveloped countries to continue studies in the South; or multiplying cooperation in health to decrease infant mortality, provide basic medical care, fight AIDS and many other actions that would only be possible if we would foster them with the solidarity necessary to ease the dark panorama of life in the South and thus face the expensive and ineffective dependency from the North?

Why not create the Debtors Fund as an elemental defence tool to have consultations and coordinate collective action policies, taking into account the full operation of the creditors forum structured by different bodies to protect their interests?

Why not advance the system of trade preferences among developing countries that only exists symbolically, whereas the protectionism of the North expels our countries from the markets?

Why not promote the compensation trade and investment flows within the South instead of competing in a suicidal fashion among us offering concessions to the multinationals of the North?

Why not establish the University of the South?

Why not create the Bank of the South?

These and other proposals retain their value and wait for our political will to become true.

But finally, dear friends, I would like to mention in particular a proposal, which, in my opinion, has great significance within this set of proposals:

In the South we are victims of the media monopoly of the North, which acts as a power system responsible for disseminating in our countries and planting in the minds of our citizens, information, values and consumption patterns that are basically alien to our realities and that have turned themselves into the most powerful and effective tool of domination. Never is domination more perfect than when the dominated people think like the dominators do.

To face and begin to change this reality, I dare to propose the creation of a TV channel that could be seen throughout the world showing information and pictures from the South. This would be the first and fundamental step to crush the media monopoly.

In a very shot time this TV channel of the South could broadcast throughout the world our own values, our own roots and tell the people in the world in the words of the great poet Mario Benedetti, a man from the deep South, Uruguay, where the La Plata River opens so much that it looks like a silver sea, and washes my dear Buenos Aires and bluish Montevideo:

"The South Also Exists"

With its French horn
And its Swedish academy
Its American sauce
And its English wrenches
With all its missiles
And its encyclopedias
Its stars war

And its opulent viciousness
With all its laurels
The North commands,
But down here
Close to the roots
Is where memory
No remembrance omits
And there are those who un-dies
And those who un-lives
And thus, all together
Work wonders
Be it known:
The South also exists.

Ladies and Gentlemen, thank you very much.

Capitalism is Savagery

[Speech at the World Social Forum, Caracas, Venezuela, January 2005.]

Ignacio Ramonet, in his introduction, mentioned that I am a new kind of leader. I accept this, especially coming from a bright mind such as Ignacio's, but many old leaders inspire me.

Some very old, like for example Jesus Christ, one of the greatest revolutionaries, anti-imperialists fighters in the history of the world, the true Christ, the Redemptor of the Poor.

Simón Bolívar, a guy that crisscrossed these lands, filling people with hope, and helping them become liberated.

Or that Argentine doctor, who crisscrossed our continent on a motorcycle, arriving in Central America to witness the gringo invasion of Guatemala in 1955, one of so many abuses that North American Imperialism perpetrated on this continent.

Or that old guy with a beard, Fidel Castro.

Abreu Lima, Artigas, San Martin, O'Higgins, Emiliano Zapata, Pancho Villa, Sandino, Morazan, Tupac Amaru, from all those old guys one draws inspiration.

Old guys that took up a commitment and now, from my heart, I understand them, because we have taken up a strong commitment. They have all returned.

Today we are millions.

One of these old guys, he was being ripped into pieces, pulled by horses from each arm and leg – Empires have always been brutal, there are no good or bad Empires, they are all aberrant, brutal, perverse, no matter what they wear or how they speak. When he felt he was about to die, he shouted, "I die today but some day I'll return and I'll be millions". Atahualpa has returned and he is millions, Tupac Amaru has returned and he is millions, Bolívar has returned and he is millions, Sucre, Zapata, and here we are, they have returned with us. In this filled up Gigantinho Stadium.

As I said two years ago here in Porto Alegre, in the third WSF, the World Social Forum is the most important political event in the world.

We have come to learn and to grasp knowledge, to soak ourselves in the passion that abounds here. We keep searching, because as every test run, the Venezuelan process needs to be monitored and improved; it is an experiment open to all the wonderful experiences happening in the world.

The World Social Forum, in these five years, has become a solid platform for debate, discussions, a solid, wide, varied, rich platform where the greater part of the excluded, those without a voice in the corridors of power, come here to express themselves and to raise their protests, here they come to sing, to say who they are, what they want, they come to recite their poems, their songs, their hope of finding consensus.

I don't feel like a President, being President is a mere circumstance. I'm fulfilling a role as many fulfill a role in any team. I'm only fulfilling a role, but I'm a peasant, I'm a soldier, I'm a man committed to this project of an alternative world which is better and possible, necessary to save the Earth. I am one more militant of the revolutionary cause.

I have been a Maoist since I entered military school, I read Che Guevara, I read Bolívar and his speeches and letters, becoming a Bolívarian Maoist, a mixture of all that.

Mao says that it is imperative, for every revolutionary, to determine very clearly who are your friends and who are your enemies.

In Latin America this is particularly important.

I'm convinced that only through the path of revolution we will be able to come out of this historical conundrum in which we have been stuck for many centuries.

The South, according to Mario Benedetti (the Uruguayan Writer) also exists. There are many revolutionaries in North America and in Europe, but although I could be wrong, I think that the South is where there is a greater conscience about the need for urgent, rapid and profound change in the World.

In 1950 we had the Summit at Bandung, where the movement of non-aligned countries was born, giving birth to the concept of the conscience of the South.

But then, with the collapse of the Soviet Union, the fall of the Berlin Wall, as Stiglitz says the "happy 90s" were upon us, we were all apparently so happy, the end of history, the technological age, and so the conscience of the south was frozen, and, as an avalanche, the proposal from the Washington consensus arrived, neocolonialism, dressed around a dubious thesis, neo-liberalism, and all those IMF policies injected with particular venom in Latin America.

Today, at the WSF, no other space more appropriate, it is opportune to say that to save the world one of the first things we need is the conscience of the South.

Re-launch the conscience of the South: it is possible that many in the North don't know this, but the future of the North depends on the South, because if we do not do what we must, if we truly do not make a better world real, if we fail, behind the marines' bayonets, behind the murderous bombs from Mr. Bush, if there is not enough strength, conscience, and organization in the south to resist the neo-imperialist attacks, if the Bush doctrine were to impose itself the world would be destroyed.

Even before the polar caps melt and entire countries became submerged under the waters, the planet would see hundreds of violent rebellions. People are not going to take peacefully the imposition of the neo-liberal model, preferring to die fighting than of hunger.

Trotsky said that every revolution needs the whip of a counterrevolution, and the counterrevolution whipped us hard, with economic, media and social sabotage, terrorism, bombs, violence, blood and death, coup d'état, institutional manipulation, international pressure, they tried to convert Venezuela into a subservient country, trying to install a transnational power above our laws, our institutions and our constitution. But the Venezuelan people demonstrated to the oligarchy that they will never surrender.

We resisted, we defended ourselves, and then went on the counteroffensive. As a result in 2003, for the first time, Venezuela recuperated its oil company, which had always been in the hands of the Venezuelan oligarchy and the North American Empire.

We were now directing almost 4 billion dollars to social investment, education, health, micro credits, housing, directed to the poorest. The neo-liberals say we are throwing money away . . . but they were giving it away to the gringos, or shared it amongst themselves in their juicy business deals.

We have called everybody to study, grandmothers, children, many of them living in misery, so we created a system to give half a million grants of 100 dollars each per month. Almost 600 million per year that before was stolen from us and now is redistributed to empower the poor so they can defeat their own poverty.

Today we also have the Missions, for example Barrio Adentro. It is a national crusade involving everybody, civilians, military, old, young, communities, the national and local governments, grassroots community organizations, helped by Revolutionary Cuba. Today there are almost 25 thousand Cuban doctors and dentists living among the poorest, plus Venezuelan male and female nurses. 50 million cases were seen during 2004 – that's double the Venezuelan population. Before, the money to pay for all this left the country.

Before, education was privatized. That's the neo-liberal, imperialist plan, health systems were privatized, that cannot be, it's a fundamental human right. Health, education, water, energy, public services, that cannot be given to the voracity of private capital, that denies those rights to the people, that's the road to savagery, capitalism is savagery.

Every day I'm more convinced, less capitalism and more socialism.

We need to transcend capitalism, but capitalism cannot be transcended from within. Capitalism needs to be transcended via socialism, with equality and justice, that's the path to transcend the capitalist power.

I'm also convinced that it's possible to do it in democracy . . . but watch it, what type of democracy . . . not the one Mr. Superman wants to impose.

Although I admire Che Guevara very much, his thesis

was not viable. His guerrilla unit, perhaps 100 men in a mountain, that may have been valid in Cuba, but the conditions elsewhere were different, and that's why Che died in Bolivia, a Quixotic figure.

History showed that his thesis of one, two, three Vietnams did not work.

Today, the situation does not involve guerrilla cells, that can be surrounded by the Rangers or the Marines in a mountain, as they did to Che Guevara, they were only maybe 50 men against 500, now we are millions, how are they going to surround us . . . Careful, we might be the ones doing the surrounding . . .

 . . . not yet, little by little.

Empires sometimes do not get surrounded, they rot from inside, and then they tumble down and get destroyed, as the Roman Empire and every Empire from Europe in the past centuries. Some day the rottenness that it carries inside will end up destroying the US Empire.

And the great people of Martin Luther King will be free, the great U.S. people, our brothers and sisters.

We are not yet declaring victory, but reality shows that the process is ongoing, although we have to nurture it every day. That's one of my sermons to my compañeros and compañeras every day. And as Che said, we need revolutionary efficacy, fighting bureaucratism and corruption.

In 2003 and 2004, we saw the strengthening of the Venezuelan economy. Manufacturing, agriculture are all growing. For the first time in a long time we can say that we don't have to import rice, we are self-sufficient in corn, and we will continue to rescue our agriculture, helping us attain food sovereignty. In the war against the latifundios, we recognize the example of the MST. They have been an example to us and to the rest of the peasants all over the continent.

In 2004 we entered Mercosur (South American Common Market). I am critical of its profile, but still we decided to join. Five years ago I was criticized for being in Canada in the Americas Summit. But I was the only one there opposing the FTAA, because it is nothing but a colonialist project. We want to create an alternative integrationist model, which we call Bolívarian alternative or ALBA [Bolívarian Alternative for Latin American and the Caribbean]. This project progresses, one would want it to be faster, but there are realities and moments, timing.

The sun rose on January 1st, 2005 and the FTAA has gone to hell. Where is the FTAA, Mr. Danger? The FTAA is dead. There are little FTAAs, but the North American Empire did not have the strength, in spite of so much pressure and blackmail, to impose on this continent the imperialist and neocolonial model that the FTAA represented. I do not want to overestimate the weakness of our adversary. It would be a fatal error. But nevertheless I think it is convenient to objectively recognize its weaknesses. Because if one believes that the adversary is unbeatable, well, it is unbeatable.

History has Vietnam, the Iraqi people resisting the attack and invasion, Revolutionary Cuba forty years later still resisting. Bolívarian Venezuela resisting for already 6 years. North American Imperialism is not invincible. Of course it is important to know that, because there are people around with good intentions who think that it is invincible and we cannot even hit it with rose petals, the Empire can get angry and react.

Goliath is not invincible. That makes it more dangerous, because as it begins to be aware of its weaknesses, it begins to resort to brute force. The assault on Venezuela, utilizing brute force, is a sign of weakness, ideological weakness.

This is not the same Latin America of even five years ago. I cannot, out of respect for you, comment on the internal situation of any other country. There in Venezuela, particularly the first two years, many of my partisans criticized me, asking me to go faster, that we had to be more radical. I did not consider it to be the right moment, because processes have stages. Compañeros, there are stages in the processes, there are rhythms that have to do with more than just the internal situation in every country, they have to do with the international situation. And even if some of you make noise, I will say it: I like Lula, I appreciate him, he is a good man, with a big heart, a brother, a compañero, and I'm sure that Lula and the people of Brazil, with Nestor Kirchner and the Argentine people, with Tabarez Vazquez and the Uruguayan people, we will open the path towards the dream of a United Latin America, different, possible.

A big hug, I love you all very much, a big hug to everybody, Many, many thanks.

[Translated by Daniel Morduchowicz.]

Socialism and Barbarism

[Speech at the 16th World Youth Festival, Caracas,
Venezuela: August 13, 2005.]

I was remembering Karl Marx and Rosa Luxemburg and the phrase that each one of them, in their particular time and context put forward: the dilemma "socialism or barbarism." Marx, the original author of this phrase, and of all the dilemmas contained in it, "socialism or barbarism," put forward that phrase looking towards a future horizon.

Afterwards, years after, Rosa Luxemburg also thought of this issue with the understanding that some day, at some moment in the not so immediate future, human beings would see ourselves in a future moment, confronted with a crossroad which would urge us to make a collective decision, a decision to change the social order to save life on this planet, to achieve survival, social progress and equality, and what is for many utopia, or on the contrary, confronted with this dilemma, this crossroad, not being capable of make real changes, we would allow the end of life on this planet, the actual survival of our species.

So, Karl Marx could reflect, think and write looking towards a distant future, a century, the same could be said of Rosa Luxemburg . . . but for us it can't. The circumstances have changed terribly. The situation today is radically different. We don't have centuries in front of us, it could be decades at most that are left for the peoples of this planet to make a decision. Or we really change the social and economic order, we give real form, viability and outlet for socialism, we say now a new, renovated socialism of the 21st century, or we decide that life finishes on this planet. We no longer have the long time that Karl Marx had, or any other fighter of that era.

This reflection is something I feel deep in my heart because of my profound conviction that the planet is being degraded more and more everyday, and that life on this planet is under threat. Because of this, today, very dilemma has returned with much more force, socialism or barbarism. I believe it is time that we take up with courage and clarity a political, social, collective and ideological offensive across the world. A real offensive that permits us to move progressively, over the next years, the next decades, leaving behind the perverse, destructive, destroyer, capitalist model and go forward in constructing the socialist model to avoid barbarism and beyond that the annihilation of life on this planet. I believe this idea has a strong connection with reality. I don't think we have much time. Fidel Castro said in one of his speeches I read not so long ago, "tomorrow could be too late, let's do now what we need to do." I don't believe that this is an exaggeration. The planet will disintegrate, society will disintegrate, the environment is suffering damage that could be irreversible, global warming, the greenhouse effect, the melting of the polar ice caps, the rising sea level, hurricanes, the terrible social occurrences that have shaken life on this planet.

Comrades, that is why I believe that in all the history of the World Festival of Youth and Students – which already has nearly 60 years, the World Federation of Democratic Youth is 60 years old and the festival has 58 years – I believe that never before has it been necessary that the festival, this festival, our festival, does not finish the day of the closing ceremony, but rather that the festival is the beginning of a new stage of conformation, of impulsion of a powerful global movement, or of strengthening, because it already exists, giving it an overall orientation in each continent, region, sub-region, bringing closer together the social movements, political movements, movements for transformation, revolutionary movements, workers, the working class, indigenous peoples, students, youth, women, thinkers, intellectuals, all of us to grow in strength. This same preoccupation, this same anguish, this same idea I transmitted last December during two significant events in Caracas. At the gathering of Artists and Intellectuals in Defence of Humanity, I commented to my friends that we cannot discuss for 100 years more, we can't spend much time debating. The debate must be permanent, but action must also be permanent. Debate must be accompanied by action and that action as according to the dialectic, must permanently feed into the debate.

It is the moment of offensive, of the masses, of struggle, of battle. It is a new moment we have now and we don't know if we will have another moment later, we don't know if we will have time. I believe there is not enough time to wait 50 years for another moment so advantageous like this one to advance the global struggle against imperialism, against imperialist hegemony and for the creation of new paths, the opening of new paths.

I also spoke at the other event to the friends of the Congress of the Bolívarian Peoples, where I proposed the creation of a type of co-ordination, a commission, a group – however we want to call it – that dedicates itself to articulating itself with movements of the whole world to initiate actions, design uniting schemes, strategies for the whole world. I have to say I am not happy with the results, yet this festival is a marvelous opportunity to insist on this point. At the World Social Forum in Porto Alegre, I once again planted this idea, because I have felt that in these events there is debate and debate and debate, sometimes there aren't even conclusions. We spend 5 days, 8 days of much happiness, meetings, hugs, but this world is under threat! We can't spend 50 more years like this, there won't be a world in 50 years if we don't stop in some way the beast that is devouring the planet and life on it!

We don't have much time in front of us, we don't have time to lose, and hopefully something will come out from this encounter. I am at your service to help in whatever way we can in this direction, all of Venezuela is at your service to continue the process everyday, without rest, this process of discussion, ideas, proposals, struggle and of battle, and so as to not only see each other at festivals every four years or every time there is a meeting of the G8 in some place where some groups go to protest. That is not enough! We need to be at it every day and every night. Either we save the world or we allow the world to be uprooted.

I remember that when I was in prison, I read an interview by Commandante Tomas Borge with Fidel Castro from 1989–90, in the midst of the collapse of the Soviet Union, in the midst of the collapse of the socialist camp. In this interview Fidel, in the middle of this darkness, it seems he could see a light and he said that soon there would be a new wave of the peoples. He referred to Latin America in particular but it is a wave across the world. And it is this precisely, that is another characteristic of the moment we are living. This characteristic, friends, comrades, could be a potential for change that we need to take advantage of.

We are faced with a new threat; we don't have time to lose. We need to arm ourselves from now with a spirit of the offensive, enough of being defensive, the best defence is attack! All the military strategies indicate that a war is never won on the defensive, you can pass to the defence to win time, this is valid in military wars, political wars and including in relationships this is valid.

Only on the offensive do you win the war, do you win the combat. What is necessary is to know how to utilize the moment, it is necessary to evaluate and create conditions. According to my criteria, we are in a moment for an offensive; we need to unleash it at a world level. I believe it has been unleashed, we need to orientate it, co-ordinate it better and we will have much better results, hopefully sooner than we expect.

I said earlier today in Teresa Carreno (theatre), you have to reproduce yourselves. No young person from any part of the world who has come can get back and unpack their luggage and take up their particular lives, their studies, their family. No, those that did that would be betraying the spirit of the festival. You have to get there to reproduce yourself, to grow and multiply.

Each one of you needs to be an importer of this (information), repeat it on the street corner and on the street, write it on the murals of the cities, on the walls of the towns and cities, repeat it in the universities, repeat it where you live, sleep, and work, in all parts, without any type of rest. Go and repeat that imperialism is not invincible, go and repeat that we are in a time of offensive, go and repeat that a new time is approaching, go and repeat in different areas that there is a threat that they need to see, hear. Go and fill them with dreams, hope and strength, the peoples you represent, that is one of the big tasks of every man and woman at this 16th festival.

The success of this festival will not be measured here in Caracas, we will see tomorrow or the day after if this festival has been useful for something, or better said if it is successful, because it has been useful for many things. For this festival, from my point of view, to say that this festival was successful, tomorrow or the day after we need to prove that it was had an impact over there in the four winds of the five continents. An impact felt with the offensive of the youth, who battle for the future because the future, said Che, belongs to us. Today we have to say that it, the future, belongs to you.

[Translated by Federico Fuentes.]